FLOATER

BY RICK AND RYAN GOLDSBERRY

Future House Publishing
FLOATER
Text copyright © 2014 by Rick Goldsberry
Illustrations copyright © 2014 by Ryan Goldsberry
All rights reserved.

To my kids and their kids -- Rick
To my kiddos: Cate, Kian, Millie, Annie and Matilda -- Ryan

ISBN: 0989125327 ISBN-13: 978-0-9891253-2-1 No part of this book may be
reproduced or transmitted in any form by any means, graphic, electronic, or
mechanical, including photocopying, recording, taping, or by any information
storage or retrieval system, without the written permission of the publisher.

My **old** life...

My **new** life...

Last night I had a wonderfully weird dream,
and when I woke up I was...

Floating...

My **brain** couldn't make up its mind.
Was this **fun** or **scary**?

Fun?

Scary?

Fun?

Scary?

Then **Mom** opened the door.

That was scary.

"Why aren't you ready
for **school?**" she asked.
"I **can't** go to school. I'm
floating," I said.
"That is **not** an excuse. You're
going to school," she said.
And then she called my best friend Alex.

Alex helped me get to school **safely**.

Sort of...

When we got to school, I remembered that it was **field trip** day.

So off we went to the ZOO.

At the ZOO, we went to see one of Alex's favorite
animals, the monkey. But it was gone. This
day was not turning out to be fun.

Alex said that since I was floating anyway, I might
get close enough to feed the animals. We bought
a bunch of peanuts, and I loaded up my pockets.

SPIDER
MONKEY

Along the way I learned some interesting animal facts.

Giraffes have bad breath.

You can't beat an **elephant** in a water fight.

And if you really want to see crocodiles become **active**, dangle something over them.

Later I saw a little kid having fun. He seemed
happy until he let go of his balloon. A cold,
scary feeling came over me.

I watched the balloon float up, up, **up.**

I yelled down to Alex:
"Whatever you do,
do not let go of me!"

"Won't happen!" Alex yelled back.
"I tied the cord from my
pants to your pants."

The balloon that had floated away
was almost gone.

Then I felt a sudden tug.

It was the monkey!

It raced **up** the cord and
began digging through my
pockets for the **peanuts.**

The **next** thing I knew...

I was **hanging**
on for dear life...
in my underwear.

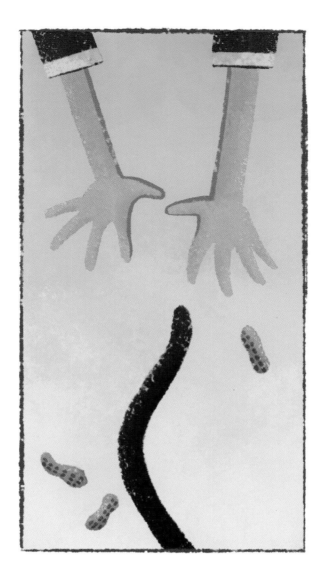

And then, the monkey slipped out of my hands.

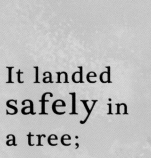

It landed
safely in
a tree;

I floated
away.

What would happen to me now? How **high** would I go?

Then, I heard a **loud** noise.

I held on to the wing
as **tightly** as I could.
I noticed a little girl.
She waved and smiled.

Did she think this was
some kind of **adventure?**
She clapped her hands and
cheered like I was a **hero.**

Then I thought something I hadn't thought before.

So I let go.

"This is an adventure!"
I yelled out loud.

And when I popped up
through the **highest
clouds,** do you know
what **I saw?**

Other **floaters!**

I bumped into a boy. "How come I stopped floating up?" I asked him.

"It's like learning to ride a **bike**," he said. "When you **stop** being afraid, that's when you can control it."

I smiled.

"And it gets **more fun** with practice," he said. "Where are your pants?"

"The Floater Retrieval Unit is here to take the **new kids** back," he said. "They haven't learned to float down yet. I can float back on my own. I'll see you **later**."

When I got home, Mom hugged me for a ridiculously long time.

"I thought I'd lost you," she said. "You can stay home from school tomorrow if you like."

"It's all right, Mom," I said. "This will get more fun with practice."

And it **did.**